S.W. Coggeshall

A Discourse delivered at the Formation of the New England Methodist Historical Society at the Bromfield St. Church, Boston

SALZWASSER
VERLAG

S.W. Coggeshall

A Discourse delivered at the Formation of the New England Methodist Historical Society at the Bromfield St. Church, Boston

Reprint of the original, first published in 1859.

1st Edition 2022 | ISBN: 978-3-37513-280-4

Verlag (Publisher): Salzwasser Verlag GmbH, Zeilweg 44, 60439 Frankfurt, Deutschland
Vertretungsberechtigt (Authorized to represent): E. Roepke, Zeilweg 44, 60439 Frankfurt, Deutschland
Druck (Print): Books on Demand GmbH, In de Tarpen 42, 22848 Norderstedt, Deutschland

Transactions of the New England Methodist Historical Society,

No. 1.

INTRODUCTION OF METHODISM INTO BOSTON.

A

DISCOURSE

DELIVERED AT THE FORMATION OF THE

New England Methodist Historical Society,

AT THE

BROMFIELD ST. CHURCH, BOSTON,

MONDAY, FEBRUARY 28, 1859,

BY

REV. S. W. COGGESHALL,

OF THE PROVIDENCE ANNUAL CONFERENCE.

"O God! we have heard with our ears,
Our fathers have told us
What deeds thou didst in their days,
In the days of old." — Ps. xliv. 1, NOYES' TRANS.

BOSTON:
PRESS OF GEO. C. RAND AND AVERY,
NO. 3 CORNHILL.
1859.

The whole of this discourse does not appear as delivered. Those portions of it which relate to the visits to Boston of CHARLES WESLEY and GEORGE WHITEFIELD, and of Messrs. BOARDMAN and BLACK, had been published in detached parts, in Zion's Herald, and the substance of which was then extemporized. The whole now appears as originally written. It has been composed with care and research; and although a small, yet I trust will not be an unacceptable contribution to the ecclesiastical history of our beloved New England.

THE AUTHOR.

DISCOURSE.

My subject for this occasion is the Introduction of
Methodism into Boston. It will constitute an entire
and not unimportant chapter in the ecclesiastical history
of the most ecclesiastical city on this continent.

A complete and well-written history of this modern
Athens — this literary emporium of the New World,
even — has not yet been produced. Snow's History,
published in 1825, is a very imperfect and unsatisfactory
production. It is a valuable repository of facts relating to
the colonial period of the history of the city, and especially of ecclesiastical matters. But it was written and published in great haste, is of no literary pretensions whatever, and, moreover, for the most part, falls off just
where the history of the city culminates, — viz., at the
Revolutionary period; so that it affords us but little information respecting matters since 1776. It has also
been long since out of print.

Drake's History, recently published, is a very different performance. It is a perfect *thesaurus* of material, is
enriched with copious and valuable notes, is highly illus-
trated and embellished, and its mechanical execution is
in the highest style of the art; is alike creditable to all
concerned, and is a valuable legacy to the public. Unlike Hildreth and some others who have essayed to

write history, Mr. Drake, either from ignorance or design, does not affect to ignore ecclesiastical facts and ecclesiastical personages. By no means. He seems desirous of giving due prominence to both. But, for certain reasons, — like Southey in his celebrated Life of Wesley, — with all his laborious research, he is, perhaps, incapable of properly appreciating the nature and relative importance of ecclesiastical affairs, and, therefore, of correctly and properly rendering the facts in the case. His work, moreover, closes where the most interesting and important period of the history of the town begins, — viz., in 1773, and just where we most need information. But Mr. Drake is a most indefatigable student in his special department; and it is to be hoped that he will continue his useful labors, and bring the History of Boston down to the present time, or, at least, to the close of our last war with Great Britain, which, in connection with Revolutionary times, constitutes one of its most important and interesting periods.

President Quincy's History of Harvard College, in two volumes octavo, is a work of great ability and of exceeding merit, and its narrative reads like a romance. But it affords us no information respecting the history of this metropolis, any further than it is connected with the affairs of that time-honored seat of learning. It is to be feared, that this valuable book, and which deserves a more extensive circulation, is but little known beyond the Unitarian denomination.

I regret, that in no one volume, nor in any number of them which have fallen into my hands, have I yet met with a fair and complete exhibit of the ecclesiastical annals of Boston, which has made it very difficult for me to present my subject in all its desirable connections. The history of the church of God, notwithstanding the great diversity of denominations into which it is divided, is a unit, and *must* be thus presented, if presented truly and correctly. I have therefore done what I could in overcoming these obstacles, and now offer you a few gleanings from this wide and interesting field.

The first Methodist who ever trod the streets of the metropolis of New England, the Queen City of the land of the Puritans, was no less a personage than Charles Wesley, the brother of John Wesley, the founder of the denomination, the poet of Methodism, and the finest hymn writer which the Christian church has yet produced.*

August 11th, 1736, after a stay of more than six months in Georgia, he sailed from Charleston, S. C., for home, in the ship London Galley, Captain Indivine. He thus introduces us to the acquaintance of this nautical worthy, to whose special keeping he had now committed his life and property, for one of the most tempestuous and dangerous voyages on record. "I found," says he, "that the honest captain had let my cabin to another. My flux and fever, that have hung upon me, forced me for some nights past to go into a bed ; but now my only bed was a chest, on which I threw myself in my boots, and was not overmuch troubled with sleep till the morning. What was still worse, I had no asylum to flee to from the captain, the most beastly man I ever saw ; a cruel, drunken, quarrelsome fool ; praying, yet swearing continually. The first sight I had of him was upon the cabin floor, stark naked and dead drunk."

---

* Some may question whether Charles Wesley can be considered a Methodist at this time. To this I reply that the rise of Methodism is dated from the formation of " The Godly Club " at Oxford in 1729, and of which Charles Wesley was an original member. And the same may be said of Mr. Whitefield, who became a member of the Club in 1735.

They met with very bad weather, even but a few days out, and towards the end of the month their perilous situation became painfully apparent. The ship was quite unseaworthy, and the miserable captain still more so. "August 28th," says he, "after a restless, tempestuous night, I hardly rose at eight. Our happier captain, having got his dose, could sleep day and night upon the stretch, and defy either pumps or squall to wake him."

"August 30th, at noon, we were alarmed at an outcry of the sailors, at their having continued pumping several hours without being able to keep the water under. They desired the captain to put into some port before they were got out to sea too far for returning; but he was too drunk to regard them. At five, the sailors came down in a body to the great cabin, waked, and told him it was as much as their lives were worth to proceed on their voyage, unless the leaks were stopped; that he remembered that it was as much as ever they could do to keep the ship above water in their passage from Boston, being forced to pump without ceasing; that the turpentine fell down upon, and closed up the pumps continually; nor was it possible for them to hold out in such continued labor, which made them so thirsty they could not live on their allowance of water; that they must come to shorter still, through his neglect to take in five hogsheads more of water, as his mate advised him; that he owned they had no candles for half the voyage. On all which accounts, they begged him to consider, whether their common safety did not require them to put in to some land for some water and candles; and above all, to stop the leaks. The captain having now slept out his rum, replied, 'To be sure, the men talk reason;' and without consulting

any of his officers, he immediately gave orders to stand
away for Boston."

"Sept. 15th. This is the first time I have heard a
sailor confess ' it was a storm.' We lay under our main-
sail and let the ship drive, being, by conjecture, about
sixty leagues from Boston on Georges' Bank, though, as
we hoped, past the shoals upon it. The captain never
troubled himself about anything, but lay snoring, even
in such a night as the last, though frequently called,
without even stirring either for sqalls, soundings or
shoals."

September 22d they made the Cape, and on the 24th
they arrived in Boston. Mr. Wesley and the passengers
came up to town in the pilot boat, "bidding a hearty
farewell," says he, "to our wretched ship, and more
wretched captain, who, for the last two days had, most
happily for us, lain dead drunk on the floor, without
sense or motion." Under God, they were indebted for
the safety of themselves and ship, to the mate, who was
an able seaman and a faithful officer.

He "remained in Boston, waiting to re-embark for
more than a month," during which time he was treated
with great kindness by several respectable residents, and
preached in two or three of the churches, with invita-
tions also to preach in the country; but with which he
was unable to comply, on account of the state of his
health.

The Episcopal churches in Boston at this time were
King's Chapel, in Common, now Tremont street, which
was the first in New England, and was organized in the
reign of James II., 1686. Its present house of worship,
however, was not erected till 1754. Also, Christ's
Church, in Salem street, constituted in the reign of the
First George, 1723, and whose church edifice was

erected the same year. It was long distinguished for having the only chime of bells in New England. Its rector, at this time, was the Rev. Timothy Cutler, formerly the rector of Yale College. Several years before he had embraced Episcopacy ; had gone to England for ordination, and on his return had accepted the pastorship of this church. He was one of the most learned and elegant scholars who adorned the annals of New England at this period — just the man to appreciate and esteem such a person as Charles Wesley. Also, Trinity Church, in Summer Street, which was constituted in 1734, two years before Charles Wesley's visit, and their church edifice, a large, plain, wooden structure, was built the year before, viz., 1735. It stood till it was superseded by the present beautiful edifice in the year 1829. Hence, there is yet standing in the metropolis of New England, and now in good repair, one church which has resounded with the voice of this elegant Oxford scholar, and one of the original members of " The Godly Club" and first poets of Methodism, and which is therefore a memorial of this extraordinary man. And what is more, the very sermons preached in these churches, are still extant, in a volume which now lies before me, published in London in 1816. One, preached in Christ's Church, Salem street, is from Ps. cxxvi. 6: " He that goeth forth and weepeth, bearing precious seed, shall doubtless come again with rejoicings, bringing his sheaves with him." Another, which was preached October 17th, was from 1 Kings xviii. 12: " And Elijah came unto all the people, and said, How long halt ye between two opinions ? If the Lord be God, then follow him ; but if Baal, then follow him." There is also another, preached on board the London Galley, on his passage from Charleston to Boston, from

Mark xii. 30 : " Thou shalt love the Lord thy God with all thy heart, and with all thy soul, and with all thy mind, and with all thy strength." And there is still another, preached on board the Simonds, on his outward bound passage to Georgia, on Phil. iii. 13, 14 : " Brethren, I count not myself to have apprehended ; but this one thing I do ; forgetting those things which are behind, and reaching forth into those things which are before, I press toward the mark for the prize of my high calling of God in Christ Jesus."

" While Mr. Charles Wesley remained at Boston," says his able biographer, Mr. Jackson, " the illness he so frequently mentions, increased, so as to cause great suffering, and even to endanger his life. He was attended by three or four physicians, among whom were Drs. Gibbons and Gardiner, of Boston, and Dr. Graves, of Charlestown, who also came to afford him advice ; yet for some days he obtained little or no relief. At one period of his illness he seems to have been apprehensive that his end was near; and he states that in his extremity he obtained spiritual strength and comfort in the use of Pascal's prayer in affliction. As the time of embarcation drew near, his friends urged him to give up all thoughts of proceeding on his voyage till his health was greatly improved. But he was deaf to their entreaties, declaring that nothing but death should hinder him from fulfilling his charge. He was entrusted with important dispatches to the Trustees of Georgia, in his official character as secretary to the governor, and Indian Affairs ; and he would neither commit them to the care of any other person, nor delay the delivery of them himself, whatever might be the effect upon his own life and health. For nothing was he more remarka-

2

ble than for noble hardihood and daring in all matters that concerned his conscience and duty."

He re-embarked October 25th. But the voyage to England proved scarcely less stormy and calamitous than had that from Charleston to Boston. But there was one happy exception. The drunken, worthless In-divine was discharged, and a new captain was shipped in his stead, and who appears to have been both intelligent and obliging; and which added greatly to the comfort of his passengers, as well as to the safety of the ship.

"October 28th, the captain," says he, "warned me of an approaching storm. In the evening, at eight, it came on, and rose higher and higher, after I thought it must have come to its height; for I did not lose a moment of it, being obliged, by the return of my flux, to rise continually. At last the long wished for morning came, but brought no abatement of the storm. There was so prodigious a sea that it quickly washed away our sheep, half of our hogs, and drowned the most of our fowls. The ship had been new calked at Boston, but how carefully it now appeared; for, being deeply laden, the sea streamed in at the sides so plentifully that it was as much as four men could do, by continual pumping, to keep her above water." Finally, they were compelled to cut away the mizzen-mast, after which the ship worked easier. December 3d, after a passage of nearly four months, he arrived safely at Deal, thankful for the divine mercies; and from which place he imme-diately proceeded to London. Here, in little more than a twelvemonth after his arrival, he received that inward baptism of the Spirit, and that endowment from on high, which sent him forth upon that glorious work

which he subsequently accomplished in the course of a
very protracted and laborious life.*

In September, 1740, just four years after the visit of
Charles Wesley, his friend and *quondam* member of the
Oxford " Godly Club," now an eloquent and flaming
herald of the cross, the Rev. Geo. Whitefield, was in
Boston, in the performance of his duty as an itinerant
evangelist. " The great awakening " under the labors
of Jonathan Edwards, and others, had now begun. Mr.
Whitefield's fame, as a preacher, had preceded him, and
although a clergyman of the Church of England, the
children of the Puritans received him with open arms,
and with most cordial greetings. A deputation of gen-
'tlemen met him, before his entrance into town, and
escorted him to his lodgings, at Mr. Staniford's, the
brother-in-law of the Rev. Dr. Colman, the senior pastor
of the Brattle Street Church. Here he preached to
immense, admiring and enthusiastic audiences, which
were moved under his appeals as the trees of the wood
are moved by a mighty wind. All classes now united
in homage to this brightest " star " of the Christian con-
stellation — all were equally lavish of their attentions,
not excepting the courtly and accomplished Belcher,
then royal governor of the province, and who sometimes
gave him a seat in his carriage. He preached in
Brattle Street, the Old South, the New North, and in
the Summer Street churches ; on a platform, outside
the meeting house of the Rev. Matthew Byles, in Hollis
Street, and on the Common. Of all these church buildings, then honored with the presence of this extraordinary man, but one, the Old South, on the corner of
Washington and Milk Streets, is now standing. The
people were almost as lavish of their money for his
Orphan House, in Georgia, for which they gave him

* Jackson's Life of Rev. C. Wesley, pp. 74—9.

immense collections, for the times,* as they were of their admiration and attentions. But what was best of all, large numbers were now awakened to a sense of their lost condition as sinners, and were made happy partakers of the pardoning mercy and the regenerating grace of God. Boston had never before seen the like, and never did again during the last century. It was an era in her history.

Whitefield was truly pious and sensible, as well as talented ; but he was yet a young man of but twenty-six ; and being now indoctrinated with the Calvinism of the New England divines, by whom he was surrounded, and with whom he was in daily contact, the adulation and the doctrine, both united, proved a little too much for him ; and at this time he sends to his old friend and former teacher, John Wesley, a man so greatly his superior in age and wisdom and learning, the following extraordinary epistle, under date of September 20th, 1740:

"Dear Brother Wesley :—What do you mean by disputing in all your letters ? May God give you to know yourself, and then you will not plead for absolute perfection, or call the doctrine of election 'a doctrine of devils.' My dear brother, take heed; see that you are in Christ a new creature. Beware of a false peace; strive to enter in at the strait gate, and give all diligence to make your calling and election sure. Remember that you are but a babe in Christ, if so much. Be humble, talk little, think and pray much. Let God teach you, and he will guide you into all truth. I love you heartily. I pray that you may be kept from error, both in principle and practice. Salute all the brethren. If you must dispute, stay till you are master of your

* For instance — £440 at Mr. Webb's, the "New North," Hanover street, and at other churches and places in proportion.

subject; otherwise you will but hurt the cause you
would defend. Study to adorn the gospel of our Lord
in all things, and forget not to pray for your affectionate
friend,   GEORGE WHITEFIELD."

Philip, Mr. Whitefield's biographer, says, "Whatever
truth there may be in this tirade, it is more than de-
fected by its unhallowed form. Such an appeal could
only exasperate." And it did exasperate. It occa-
sioned an estrangement between the parties, then the
leaders in the great revival which had now commenced
on both sides of the Atlantic, which, although reason
and religion being permitted to be heard in the case,
was eventually removed, yet proved productive of un-
happy consequences, as all such things must do. And
even Tracy, the author of the "Great Awakening,"* in
giving an account of Whitefield's present visit to Boston,
and in commenting on this celebrated admonition letter,
adds:—"Scarce any writer has mentioned it but in a
similar style of condemnation; and it was certainly an
improper letter to be addressed by a very young man
to a minister of the gospel so much his superior in age
and acquirements, of established reputation for piety,
and who had so long been the spiritual guide of the
author. Whitefield would not have written it, had he
not been — to use his own language on another occasion — 'puffed up' by his reception and success at
Boston."

Mr. Whitefield also, at this time, preached in Roxbury, Cambridge, Charlestown, Salem, Ipswich, Newburyport and Portsmouth, N. H., from which he proceeded as far as York, Me., to visit the Rev. Samuel
Moody, the pious and venerable, but eccentric, pastor
of the church in that place. On his return, he passed
through the province to Northampton, to visit Edwards,

* Pp. 92, 98.

then the Corypheus of the New England clergy, among whose people the revival had commenced six years before. Pleased with the appearance of Edwards' church, yet the scene of a great work, as well as with the appearance of his household, which was the scene of great domestic happiness, possessed, as he was, of one of the most beautiful, accomplished and pious women in New England, he pronounced them " a sweet couple;" and thence proceeds down the valley of the Connecticut, preaching incessantly as he goes; and from thence he hastens to New York.

Whitefield subsequently visited New England several times, viz., in 1745, 1756, 1764, and 1770. During the latter visit, he suddenly died in Newburyport, Mass., Sept. 30th, aged 56 years. He was buried in his dress, wig and gown, under the pulpit of the first Presbyterian Church in that ancient town, where the mortal remains of this great "master of assemblies" still rest, and in which a beautiful monument to his memory has been built. But his works, which are his greatest and most enduring monument, die not. They still live and flourish more than ever, on both sides of the Atlantic. It was his request that his earliest religious friend, Mr. Wesley, should preach his funeral sermon, and which he did in both of Mr. Whitefield's chapels in London, that in Tottenham-court-road, and also that at Moorfields, to immense audiences, from Num. xxiii., 10: " Let me die the death of the righteous, and let my last end be like his." He also preached the same sermon at several other places; remarking in his journal, " In every place I wish to show all possible respect to the memory of that great and good man."

Scarce had the eloquent voice of Whitefield been hushed in death, when God sent a Wesleyan Methodist

to Boston, to proclaim the doctrines of free grace, and
to reiterate the now almost forgotten teachings of the
great evangelist, on the new birth. This was Mr. Richard
Boardman, an Irishman by birth, an humble name, not
possessing the brilliancy or the historic fame of either
of the two former distinguished men, but a name red-
olent with the sweets of a lovely and unaffected piety,
and one of the first in the annals of American Methodism. He was one of Mr. Wesley's first missionaries to
this Western continent.

Under date of 1769, Mr. Wesley says, in his Ecclesiastical History :—" Tuesday, Aug. 1st, our Conference
began at Leeds. On Thursday I mentioned the case of
our brethren at New York. For several years past,
several of our brethren from England and Ireland, and
some of them preachers, had settled in North America,
and had formed societies in various places, particularly
Philadelphia and New York. The society in New York
had lately built a commodious preaching-house, and now
desired our help, being in great want of money, but
much more of preachers. Two of our preachers,
Richard Boardman and Joseph Pillmore, willingly offered themselves for the service, by whom we deter-
mined to send over fifty pounds as a token of our
brotherly love."

These gentlemen arrived in Philadelphia upon the
24th of October following, and immediately entered
upon their appropriate work, one taking his station in
Philadelphia, where a large and commodious house,
still in use, had been secured for the occupancy of
the society, and the other in New York. They were
assisted by Philip Embury, Robert Strawbridge, Robert
Williams, and Capt. Thomas Webb, of the British army,
local preachers, who were in the country before them,

and who had already formed societies in at least three of the provinces, viz., New York, Pennsylvania and Maryland.

Oct. 27, 1771, Francis Asbury and Richard Wright also arrived in Philadelphia, after a passage of fifty-five days, from Bristol, England. Bristol was then one of the principal places of trade with the Colonies, and consequently the usual place of embarcation for the New World. A master spirit had now come, and a new era in the history of the infant cause was now about to be inaugurated. The work was soon enlarged.

April 2, 1772, these four met in Philadelphia and agreed upon a plan of operations, which was, that Mr. Boardman should go to Boston, Mr. Pillmore to the South, Mr. Wright to New York, and that Mr. Asbury should stay in Philadelphia for three months. " With this," says the latter, " I was well pleased."

In accordance with this judicious arrangement, Mr. Pillmore at once departed for the South, and went as far as Savannah, Geo. He met with great encouragement, and was absent a year. Mr. Boardman also departed for his new field of labor; and now, after the lapse of thirty-six years since Charles Wesley had lifted up his voice in the Episcopal churches of Boston, one of his co-laborers from the Old World appears in the metropolis of New England, as the herald of a free salvation, and as the representative of the rising sect. The richly evangelical hymns of the poet of Methodism were now to be heard among the sons of the Puritans, as his classical sermons once had been.

Religion was now at a low ebb in the town of Boston. But, besides all this, the minds of the people were exceedingly engrossed with politics, which, in consequence of attempts to enforce the " Writs of Assistance " and the hated and obnoxious Stamp Act, and other high-handed and ill-judged measures of the Home Government, were rapidly assuming a most serious aspect. The British troops were already quartered in the town, the hateful presence of which, together with their massacre of citizens in State Street two years before, and the exceedingly unpopular acts of the royal governors, Barnard and Hutchinson, had influenced the minds of the Bostonians to the highest pitch of excitement.

Of the precise time that Mr. Boardman arrived in Boston, how long he remained, how he was particularly received and treated by the people, and what was the exact amount of his success, we have now no means of knowing. That, under the above circumstances, he should meet with any success at all in his mission of love to the children of the Pilgrims, is almost wonderful. But, as is generally the case with the zealous and indefatigable Methodist itinerant, he *did* meet with success. Obtaining the use of a place of worship, he preached a free salvation to all who came to hear, and not in vain. Some believed the word, were happily converted to God, and, in accordance with the usages of Methodism, were formed into a society.*

But this infant society of Wesleyans was doomed to a sudden extinction. Such was the distance of Boston from Philadelphia, then the centre of operations, and the want of facilities for travel, so unlike those of the present day; such was the great scarcity of preachers, and such, especially, were the increasing political troubles of the times, consequent upon the passage of the Boston Port Bill, by which the town was shut up about this

---

* Mr. Wesley's Missionaries to America, p. 21.

time, and which was soon after succeeded by the battles
of Lexington and of Bunker Hill, the siege of the town
by the American army under Washington, and the subsequent long and protracted war, and the fearful dis-
tresses consequent upon it, that this little society was
prevented from receiving that attention necessary to its
existence and prosperity. Some of its members, probably, were scattered in the troubles of the times, being
as sheep without a shepherd; others may have back-
slidden, while others, perhaps, may have placed themselves under the care of Dr. Stillman, an eminently
spiritual and talented minister, then pastor of the First
Baptist Church in Salem Street, from the altar of which
shone no dim or uncertain light.

A mournful and mysterious interest hangs over the
fate of this infant society in the dim distance of the
past. What were the names of its members, who were
its leaders, and who composed its board of stewards, if
it had any, are wholly unknown to us. But we trust
that the names of some, at least, were duly recorded in
the Lamb's Book of Life, never to be blotted out, and
that they will be read to the assembled and elect church
in the great day.*

Twelve long and eventful years — years of tears and
bloodshed, embracing the entire period of our American
Revolution, together with the events which immediately
preceded and followed it, — passed away, when behold!
another Wesleyan preacher, from an opposite direction,
appears in the town of Boston, to make a far deeper
and more widely spread impression than Boardman;

---

* Mr. Boardman came by the way of Newport, R. I. And in the "Old Book" of the
Trustees and Stewards of the old John Street Church, N.Y., and upon which Rev. J. B.
Wakely founded his highly interesting volume, "The Lost Chapters," under date of
May 14, 1772, is the following entry: "To cash paid Mr. Richard Boardman, passage
to Rhode Island, £1. 9. 0." — Lost Chapters, p. 203.

but almost as quickly to pass away. This was the Rev. William Black, of Nova Scotia.

Mr. Black was an Englishman by birth; and in 1775 he sailed from Hull, England, with his parents, and settled in Nova Scotia. As early as 1781 he began to preach, and formed several small societies in that distant Province, which was then crowded with political refugees from the United States, who had been compelled to leave by the troubles of the times. Not being able to take care of all these societies alone, and to enter all the new fields of labor which were constantly opening to him, the year after the conclusion of peace, in 1784, he came to the States for assistance, and was at the organization of the M. E. Church, at the famous Christmas Conference, in Baltimore of this year. His mission was successful. From this Conference, the Rev. Freeborn Garrettson, and the Rev. James O. Cromwell were sent to his help. They embarked for their new and distant field of labor in February, probably from Boston, and remained there two years, during which they placed Methodism upon a firm foundation; and it has ever since flourished in that important Province.

On Mr. Black's way to Baltimore, in the fall of 1784, he preached twice in Boston, as also in Stratfield and Norwalk, Conn., on Long Island, and in the City of New York. On his return, he did not reach Boston till February 1, 1785. None of the ministers of the town being willing to open their pulpits to this youthful stranger, he preached in private houses. First, in a chamber at the North End, and which the people so crowded that the floor sank an inch or two. He then preached in a large room at the South End. But here, in time of prayer, one of the beams of the floor broke,

" and the people screamed," says he, " as if going to be
swallowed up by an earthquake." After this, by per-
mission of the Committee, he preached two or three
times in Dr. Stillman's meeting-house — a very plain,
but large and commodious house. But as this was likely
to occasion a quarrel between the worthy Doctor, who
had some objection, and the Committee, he declined to
meet there any more. His friends then procured from
the selectmen the use of the North Latin School House;
"but neither would this contain one half the people ;"—
and one of the beams here also giving way, the people
were terribly afraid, and screamed as if about to be
crushed to death." The Sandamanian Chapel, which
stood in the rear of Hanover street, was the next procured, and was the usual place of meeting for the
remainder of his stay in town. But even this would
not contain half the people who flocked to hear the
word. The last Sabbath of his stay, he preached in Dr.
Eliot's meeting-house, the "New North," so called, on
the corner of Clark and Hanover streets, and, as he
supposed, to two thousand people; but even this, he
thought, would not have held them, if they had had
timely notice. Dr. Eliot, who thus favored our youthful evangelist, was a most excellent and estimable man,
much given to historical studies, one of the founders of
the Massachusetts Historical Society, and the author
of a Biographical Dictionary, which bears his name.
He was now, comparatively, a young man, and had become the pastor to this church, as successor to his
father, in 1779, six years before.

Mr. Black remained in Boston till May, a period of
six months, when he sailed for Cumberland, N. S., to
resume his work at home. During this time the Lord
reached the hearts of many, who found peace in believ-

ing. Now was the time for the formation of a large and flourishing society, and Mr. Black accordingly wrote to Bishop Asbury, informing him of his successes and of the promising state of the cause, and requesting him to send on preachers, to take charge of the good work begun. But Bishop Asbury was then on his tour in the South, and our postal arrangements not being so perfect and reliable as now, these letters never reached him, and no help was sent to these waiting and expectant converts. Being thus left as sheep without a shepherd, they mostly joined the Rev. Dr. Stillman's, where they found the greatest congeniality of views and feelings, and which thereby received a valuable accession both to its numbers and its piety. But there is proof that they did not thus do until all hope of obtaining the desired help had expired; for in the records of the Selectmen of Boston, under date of September 16, 1785, there is an entry, that "the use of the North Latin School House be allowed the hearers of Mr. Wm. Black, until further order."*

Thus this favorable opportunity was lost, and thus failed the second attempt to plant Methodism in the city of the Puritans. A third attempt, although under great and increasing disadvantages, was next to be made by one of the most persevering and indefatigable men, and which, in opposition to immense discouragements, was to be crowned with complete success. This eminent and distinguished laborer we will next introduce to notice.

May 28th, 1789, but a few weeks after the inauguration of Washington as the first President of the Republic, and the organization of the new Federal Government, and while Congress was engaged in its preliminary busi-

---

* Life of Rev. William Black. Also, Life of Rev. Joseph Snelling, pp. 9–10.

ness in New York, a Conference was held in that city, the second since the war. Bishops Coke and Asbury were both present; and although this Conference was composed of scarcely twenty members, yet, in piety, in talents, in eminent executive ability, and in historic fame, it has probably not been exceeded by any which has since met, however large. The session of this Conference is also distinguished for four things which will always make it prominent in our denominational annals. — 1. For having presented the first congratulatory address to Washington, after his inauguration, of any ecclesiastical body in the country, and which example was immediately followed by others: an event not without its significance and influence in those eventful days; 2. The reception, on probation, of the man, Wm. Losee, who, two years after, penetrated the wilderness of Western New York, crossed the waters of Lake Ontario, and introduced Methodism into Canada, where it has since so exceedingly flourished; 3. The permanent establishment of our Book Concern, and which has grown to its present colossal proportions; 4. The appointment of a missionary, the Rev. Jesse Lee, to New England.*

Mr. Lee entered upon his work in the town of Norwalk, Ct., on the 17th of June, by a sermon from John iii. 7, — "Ye must be born again," which was preached in the open highway, no house being opened for

---

* Although Bishop Asbury did not possess the profound learning and the varied accomplishments of Wesley, yet he was far better read in the grand science of human nature than he. Mr. Wesley was often deceived in men; Bishop Asbury, never. In the selection of agents for his work, he possessed all the sagacity of Napoleon; and, like that great commander, when he had selected them, he could inspire them with his own energy and courage, and then send them forth to the zealous and efficient performance of their work. It was one of his rules of action *to trust young men.* As they are able and willing to work, he esteemed them as not so likely to fail as old men. Hence, when he sent Lee into New England, there to lay the massive foundations of Methodism, he was but thirty-one years of age, had been in the itinerancy but six years, and though eligible, yet, from choice, was not even in elder's orders!

his use. After listening to this discourse, some of his hearers thought that such a man had not visited New England since the days of Whitefield; in which opinion they were, indeed, correct. And yet they stood aloof from him. But, nothing daunted by the coolness of this reception, all unused to it as he was, he proceeded in the labors of his important mission; and, in the face of almost insuperable difficulties and almost insurmountable obstacles, which might have discouraged a man of a less indomitable spirit, he soon formed an extensive circuit, including a large number of towns situated in the southwestern corner of the State, in the counties of Fairfield and New Haven. He labored alone till the following February, when the Rev. Lemuel Smith, Jacob Brush, and George Roberts came to his assistance, from the South. Messrs. Smith and Roberts, especially, were men who subsequently made their mark upon the religious history and character of New England, and who long lived in the affectionate remembrance of her people. Upon receiving this wished-for accession to his strength, our indefatigable laborer " thanked God, and took courage; " and, leaving Messrs. Brush and Roberts to attend to the work which he had already laid out, he took Mr. Smith, and immediately proceeded to form a new circuit, of two weeks, extending along the post road from Milford, on the Sound, to Hartford. In the spring, still another was formed, extending from the city of Middletown, on both sides of the Connecticut, to Wilbraham, Mass., called the Hartford circuit. It is worthy of remark, that the two oldest literary institutions now in existence in the Methodist Episcopal Church — the Wesleyan University at Middletown, and the Wesleyan Academy at Wilbraham — are both within the bounds of this old circuit.

The year before Mr. Lee's appointment to New England, viz., in 1788, a large district was formed, extending along the Hudson, from the city of New York to the waters of Lake Champlain, and was placed in the care of the Rev. Freeborn Garrettson. Under his able and efficient superintendence, it was in a flame of revival, and in a highly flourishing state, in the course of a single year. Under the labors of some of his preachers, who extended their work across the State line for this purpose, several small societies were formed about this time in Litchfield County, in the western part of Connecticut.

In the summer of 1790, Mr. Garrettson placed his eye upon Boston, and resolved to visit it on a tour of observation. Taking with him his body-servant, black Harry, who was a local preacher, he passed over into Connecticut, visiting these little societies before mentioned, and then to Hartford, where he preached. From thence he passed up the valley of the Connecticut, and entered the heart of Massachusetts. At Worcester, he called upon the late Dr. Bancroft, the father of the historian, then pastor of the Congregationalist Church in that ancient town, and subsequently a leader among the Unitarians. With him he took a cup of tea, and over which no grace being said, it greatly shocked the pious feelings of our Methodist itinerant, and who was not slow to remonstrate against the seeming impiety. The next day he proceeded to Boston. He says : "We rode through a very pleasant country. I never saw more elegant buildings in a country place than those which surround Cambridge ; and the college has an imposing appearance. I got into Boston about seven o'clock, after riding forty-eight miles. I boarded Harry at the master mason's, for the Africans. I took my own lodgings with a private gentleman, who had been a Methodist in England, but has, I fear, fallen from the spirit of Methodism.

"Sunday, July 14th. — I attended church in the morning, and gave great uneasiness to the people with whom I lodged, on account of my not communing. I never in my life saw such a set of communicants, dressed in the height of the mode, and in all the frippery of fashion; so much of the world in their manner and appearance, that my mind was most uneasy to look upon. In the afternoon I preached in a meeting-house which had formerly belonged to Dr. Mather; Monday evening, likewise, in the same place. Tuesday, I went from end to end of the town, and visited several who were friendly, and a few of whom were formerly Methodists, but I fear that they are now not such in practice. I engaged the use of the meeting-house, and a place for a preacher to board, and on Wednesday set out for Providence." *

This meeting-house, which had belonged to Dr. Samuel Mather, the son of the famous Cotton Mather, was the old house which formerly stood on the corner of Bennet and Hanover streets. The church was formed in 1742, principally by members from the Second Church, in North Square, and as one of the fruits of the opposition to the great revival of that period, and its house of worship was built the same year. It never had but one pastor, Dr. Mather, and who was formerly one of his father's successors at the Second Church, and colleague of the Rev. Joshua Gee. Upon his death, at a very advanced age, in 1785, by his advice, the church was merged in the Seventh Church, Hanover street, and thus became extinct. The meeting-house soon after passed into the hands of the Universal-

* Life of Garrettson, p. 192.

4

ists, under the Rev. John Murray, and immediately became the stronghold of this doctrine in New England. As Mr. Murray had formerly been a Methodist in Ireland, and still entertained an affection for his first and earliest religious friends, the Methodists were often admitted to it, at this period. This house, thus identified with the history of three denominations, and with two of the most important periods in the ecclesiastical annals of our country, was taken down but a few years since, to give place to the present larger and more imposing structure.*

But while Garrettson had thus approached Boston in one direction, Lee, who had already placed his keen and penetrating eye upon the same spot, was approaching it from another. Starting from Hartford, about the same time, he passed through Bolton, Windham, New London, and Stonington, in the eastern part of Connecticut; thence, across the waters of the Narragansett, to Newport, R. I., and from thence through Bristol and Warren to Providence, preaching as he passed along. The Sabbath that Garrettson spent in Boston, Lee was in Providence, and preached in the little State-house, yet standing; and the same day that the one left Boston for Providence, the other left Providence for Boston; and in the sweat and dust of a hot July day, they suddenly and unexpectedly encountered each other on the road, between these two places. While sitting on their horses, engaged in conversation, a gentleman of the neighborhood was passing, and seeing two respectable and interesting-looking strangers, one of them attended by a black servant, thus engaged, he stopped, introduced himself, and courteously invited them to enjoy the hospitalities of his house, which invitation they most gladly accepted,

* In 1838.

for the purpose of further consultation respecting their work. But, not satisfied with this, although it was in the midst of the haying season, in the true spirit of the laborious itinerants of those days, they were instant, in season and out of season, and preached morning and evening. The next day, after dinner, they took leave of each other and of their kind host, and each proceeded to his point of destination, — Garrettson for Providence, and thence to his immense district on the Hudson, and Lee for the capital of the Old Bay State.

Friday, July 9th, weary and toil-worn, Lee passed over the same road, leading over the " Neck," over which Washington and his troops had passed in March, 1776, and entered that far-famed town upon which his anxious and expectant eyes had been steadily fixed for the five years past. Of the meeting-house which Garrettson had engaged for his occupancy, we hear nothing. "A change had come over the spirit of the dream" of those having charge of it, for no place of meeting was now to be had, and every effort to obtain one was fruitless. But a Methodist is usually at no loss for a place in which to hold forth the Word of Life ; and Lee, especially, was not the man to be daunted by any obstacles of this kind. As Whitefield had done in the same place just fifty years before, he resolved to deliver his message in the open air. On Saturday he accordingly gave notice of his intention to preach on the Common in the afternoon of the next day, at six o'clock. At the time appointed, there were but few present; but he took his stand on a table, and commenced singing one of his familiar Methodist hymns. He had an excellent and well-trained voice, of great compass and power, and the neighboring streets soon poured forth their masses ; and when he commenced his sermon, a living crowd of between two and three thousand gave solemn attention to the commanding voice of this interesting stranger. Others, although having command of large and spacious city churches, have since thought it proper to follow his example, for the sake of gaining access to the multitude who never enter a place of worship.

On Monday, Mr. Lee left Boston, and visited Salem, Marblehead, Danvers, Ipswich, Newburyport, and other places within the bounds of old Essex. At the latter place, with feelings of devout interest, in company with the Rev. Mr. Murray, then the pastor of the First Presbyterian Church in that ancient town, he visited the tomb of the eloquent Whitefield, of which he gives an interesting account. From thence he crossed the waters of the Merrimac, and proceeded to Portsmouth, N. H., where, in the Rev. Mr. Walton's congregation, he found hungry and attentive hearers, and was favored with an interesting and profitable visit; and on the following Saturday he was again in Boston. During this week, although at midsummer, he rode one hundred and thirty miles, and preached ten times, — mostly making his own appointments. Among those who received him with especial favor at this time, was the Rev. Joshua Spaulding, then pastor of the Tabernacle Church in Salem, in whose spacious church he preached, both going and coming. Mr. Spaulding was one of those few men in New England at this period who still possessed the spirit and power of the old Puritans, and whose personal influence, even at this distance of time, is yet felt in that opulent city.

No place being yet open to him in Boston, the next day Mr. Lee again preached on the Common, to nearly three thousand persons. During this week he also preached once in a vacant Baptist meeting-house, and which, I suppose, was the Second Baptist Church, in Baldwin Place; once in a private house; and once, also, in Charlestown. On the following Sabbath, although it had rained during the day, and the ground was quite wet, he again preached on the Common, to an increasing multitude, which he estimated at five thousand. " Blessed be God!" says he, after one of these services, " he made his quickening presence known, and met us in the fields." " He had now fulfilled the object of his missionary tour, and prepared to return to his regular field of labor," but to return to Boston in the course of a few months, and to make a permanent stand.*

Oct. 4th, 1790, after the autumn leaves had begun to fall, and the forests of New England to put forth the resplendent and variegated foliage of the season, Lee entered the Conference-room in the old John-street Church, in the city of New York, fresh from his romantic labors and brilliant successes in the land of the Pilgrims, with the welcome news of one chapel built, and three circuits formed in one State; explorations made in three others for future operations, especially in Eastern Massachusetts; and nearly two hundred members in society. At one time during this session, he was closeted with Bishop Asbury for three hours, in which he gave him an account of his past labors and successes, his plans for future operations, and solicited laborers for this interesting and important field, and not in vain. Five were appointed to New England, — himself to Boston, with the presiding eldership of the others.

Immediately after the close of this Conference, he received the mournful intelligence of the death of his sainted mother, in Virginia. This sad news impressed him most painfully. " I was much confused in my

---

* Memoirs of Lee, by Minton Thrift, pp. 152–7.

mind," says he, "scarcely knowing whether it would be best for me to return to New England, or to go home. I tried to give myself to God in prayer, and to beg for instruction." Finally, it was concluded that it would be best for his brother John, who had been appointed to the New Haven circuit, to return to Virginia, and for himself to go to Boston, according to appointment. On the 15th, his brother left for his home in Sussex, in the Old Dominion. "I went with him to the ferry," says he, "and stood and looked after him for a while, and then returned with a sorrowful heart. Parting with him was almost as distressing as my mother's death."

Burying the sorrows of his great heart, and exiling himself from his loved home in the sunny South for a while longer, this moral hero turns his face unflinchingly to the East. On the 19th he left the city, and, after preaching in numerous places in Connecticut, and which were under his care as presiding elder, he took his station in Boston on the 13th of November. And now commences a series of labors and struggles, of defeats and reverses, before which almost any but the persistent and indomitable spirit of Lee might have quailed. But these defeats and disasters were presently to disappear, and these labors and struggles were finally to be crowned with success. But before I proceed to detail these events, I will first show the ecclesiastical *status* of Boston at this period, when Lee thus entered it.

The town of Boston, as strange as it may seem to us in these growing times, when even cities are built in a few years, and when that ancient metropolis is now in so flourishing a condition, had not only gained nothing in its population for the preceding fifty years, but had lost much: —

Its population in 1742 was 16,382
"   "   ". 1752 " 15,731
"   "   " 1765 " 15,520

Thus, instead of doubling its population in twenty-three years, which is according to the usual ratio of increase in this country, it actually lost 862.

Again : —

Its ratable polls in 1738 were 3,395
"   "   "   " 1741 " 2,972
"   "   "   " 1784 " 1,141

— but a fraction more than one-third as many as forty-six years before. We are not to suppose that the actual population of the town at this latter period was so small as these figures seem to indicate. A large proportion of the population, undoubtedly, were women and children, as is the case with the town of Nantucket at the present time, and for similar reasons.

In order to understand this, we are to remember that, during this preceding period of fifty years, the town had largely assisted to fit out one great naval and military expedition, — that against Louisburg, of 1745. It had passed through the old French War of 1756–63, for the support of which, at one time, its real estate was taxed to the amount of two-thirds of its value; as also that of the Revolution, from 1775 to 1783, during which it had also suffered incredibly. Its port, upon which it almost wholly depended, had been shut up by the British Government before the war, and its flourishing commerce was thus destroyed, and its people were reduced to ruin and misery. It was occupied by the British troops at the commencement of the war, as also for some time previously. It also endured the horrors of a

siege from June, 1775, to March, 1776, when, upon its
sudden evacuation by the British troops, 2,000 of its in-
habitants, attached to the royal cause, with tears and
lamentations at leaving their cherished homes, went
with them. But these were but "the beginning of sorrows." Seven long years of heavy taxation, with loss
of business, with blood and carnage, were yet before
them. No marvel, therefore, that it came out of this
war utterly prostrate and exhausted. These wars had
made fearful havoc with its male population. But a
third as many strong and able-bodied men could be seen
in the streets as fifty years before. The prosperity of
Boston in the colonial period of its history culminates
at the close of the third decade of the eighteenth century. But at this time (1790), with its growing commerce, now under the fostering care of the new Federal
Government, it had begun to rise out of its long series
of misfortunes and disasters.

The following will enable us to better understand
both the past history and the present condition of the
churches of Boston at this period : —

Of the Congregationalists. — The First Church, formed
in 1630; its house of worship, built in 1713, stood at the
lower end of Washington street, opposite the old State
House. It was a large three-story building, after the
style of the times, and was called the "Old Brick." It
was vacated for the present church in Chauncy place in
1808, and was pulled down.

The Second Church, constituted in 1649, and of which
the celebrated Mathers, father and son, had been the
distinguished pastors, had become extinct. Its house of
worship, which stood in North Square, then the court
end of the town, and near the present Mariners' Church,
was pulled down by the British soldiery, for fuel, in the

fearful winter of 1776; and in 1779 it became merged in the Seventh Church, in Hanover street, and which, hence, took its name.

The Third, the "Old South," was constituted in 1669. Its spacious house of worship, and which was in the height of the style for the times, was built in 1730, and is the only Congregationalist Church of that period which is yet standing. Sewell and Prince were its able pastors in the time of the "Great Awakening," and of which it was the headquarters in the metropolis. Old Governor Winthrop's house stood a few rods north, on the same side of the street.

The Fourth, in Brattle street, was constituted in 1699, and, from a document put forth in defence of the novel principles upon which it was organized, was called "The Manifestoe Church." The venerable Dr. Colman was its first pastor, and the Coopers, father and son, his successors. Its house of worship, yet standing, was built in 1773.

The Fifth, called the "New North," was constituted in 1714, and its house of worship, which stood on the corner of Hanover and Clark streets, was built the same year. It was one of the chief centres of interest and of attraction in the great revival of 1740–45. Its present edifice was erected in 1804. Dr. John Eliot, before mentioned, was now its pastor.

The Sixth, called the "New South," was constituted in 1716, and its house of worship, which stood in Summer street, was dedicated Jan. 8th, 1717. The beautiful octagon church, now Dr. Dewey's, which now occupies its site, was built in 1814.

The Seventh was in Hanover street. Its house of worship, which was a large three-story brick structure, and which was called the "New Brick," was dedicated

May 10, 1721. The church, however, was not gathered till May 23, 1722. It arose out of an opposition to the settlement of the Rev. Peter Thatcher as colleague of Rev. Mr. Webb at the "New North," in 1720. The cock perched on the top of the steeple, and which still, after the lapse of a hundred and thirty-eight years, holds his place on the beautiful and lofty spire of the new church, was originally placed there by Mr. Thatcher's implacable opponents in derision of his name, Peter. This church now represented three, the Second and Tenth being merged in it. And it is indeed singular that the first Methodist church planted in Boston, by Lee, and which now possesses the last house of worship built by this triple church, and around which cluster so many interesting historic associations, is its legitimate representative. Its house of worship is the most costly church edifice in New England. The church itself now meets in Bedford street.*

The Eighth, or Hollis-street Church, was constituted in 1732, and its first house of worship was built the same year. The present spacious structure was erected in 1811. This church has been rendered famous by the names of the venerable and eccentric Mather Byles,

---

* This church, which, since the sale of its large and beautiful house of worship in Hanover street to the Methodists, now meets in Bedford street, calls itself the Second Church. This is hardly in accordance with historic verity, though the reasons for it are obvious enough. The names of the two Mathers, father and son, who were among its former pastors, and of Sir William Phipps, and others who were its members, have given it a historic celebrity perhaps exceeding that of any other church in New England. And while ardent piety, extensive learning, marvellous industry, great Christian activity, and eminent public usefulness, extending down through whole generations, are things to be admired and applauded, and so long as our sturdy English tongue is read and spoken among the nations, so long must that church have a most distinguished place not only in the ecclesiastical, but also in the political, history of our growing country. But the Seventh Church will not compare with it in this respect, and possesses scarcely any historic celebrity at all, except what it may derive from the names of Henry Ware and of Ralph Waldo Emerson, who were its pastors in more recent times. But they are at liberty, I suppose, to call their church by whatever name they please.

who was for many years its first pastor, and by that of
the Rev. John Pierpont, who was one of its last.

The Ninth, or Lynde-street Church, also called the
West Church, from its location in the west part of the
town, was formed Jan. 3, 1736. It was the first in that
part of the town, now so populous. Its present house
of worship was built in 1806.

The Tenth, as before stated, was gathered in 1742;
and its house of worship, a plain wooden structure, which
stood on the corner of Hanover and Bennet streets, was
built the same year. This church has but a brief history. It never had but one pastor, the Rev. Samuel
Mather, D. D.; and upon his death in 1785, it became
extinct, its members merging themselves in the Seventh,
which now represented three, — the Second, Seventh,
and Tenth. The house soon after passed into the hands
of the Universalists, under the Rev. John Murray, who
now occupied it.

The Eleventh was formed in 1748, as one of the fruits
of the "Great Awakening" of that period. Its house
of worship had formerly belonged to the French Protestant Church, which had now become extinct. Upon the
death of its aged pastor, the Rev. Andrew Croswell, in
1785, this church also became extinct, and its house of
worship passed into the hands of the Catholics. A Universalist church now occupies its site, in School street.

The Twelfth was the Federal street. This was originally a Presbyterian Church, formed, like most others of
that period, by immigrants from Ireland, in 1729. Its
house of worship, standing at this time, had been built
in 1744. It was in this house that the Convention for
Massachusetts which adopted the Federal Constitution,
in 1788, held its session. Hence, the present name of
the street, which was before called Long lane. Its

present house of worship, long the scene of the labors of the late distinguished Wm. Channing, D. D., was built in 1809. The church had become Congregational upon the death of its last Presbyterian pastor, about 1786, and Dr. Bellamy was called to be its pastor.

Thus the Congregationalists had two churches less than forty years before. And so rapid and thorough had been the working of the Unitarian leaven among these churches, in the mighty reaction after the "Great Awakening," that but one of them maintained its adherence to the doctrines of the Westminster Confession; and so equivocal was the position of this church even, upon this subject, that when, in a great revival among the Baptists, under Stillman and Baldwin, in 1803, it felt its quickening influence, and some of its pious members proposed that the house should be opened for evening meetings, the pewholders promptly voted down the proposition. Upon this, eight of them formed themselves into a "Society for Religious Improvement;" and so destitute were even these good men of "spiritual gifts," that there was not one of them who could lead his brethren in devotional exercises. It was out of this society that the Park-street Church subsequently arose, in 1809; and all the other Orthodox-Congregational Churches in the city may be traced to this origin. Thus was Puritanism, after a hundred and eighty years, compelled to rebuild, almost from the foundation, in its own chosen seat. Was there no need for Lee's evangelical labors here at this time ?*

* I have taken this from Moore's "Boston Revival of 1842," p. 28, and whose text I have here strictly followed. But I would here inform Mr. Moore, and those who seek their information from him and from similar sources, that there was not only a Methodist Church in this city at that time, but also a young Methodist preacher, the Rev. Thomas Lyell, who, although, on account of his youth, in points of weight of character and theological learning, probably inferior to Drs. Stillman and Baldwin, the pious and able pastors of the Baptist churches at this time, — yet, in pulpit oratory and

At this time, also, the Rev. Thomas Foxcroft, the colleague of Dr. Chauncy, in the First Church; Joshua Gee, of the Second; the pious and fervent Sewall, and his colleague, the scholarly and elegant Prince, of the "Old South;" the venerable Dr. Colman, and his two colleagues and successors, the two Coopers, father and son, of the Brattle-street Church; John Webb, and his colleague, the amiable Dr. Andrew Eliot, of the New North; Samuel Checkley, of the New South, Summer street; as well as others who had welcomed Whitefield in 1740, as well as upon his subsequent visits, and who had been so active and useful in the great revival of former years, — were now all gathered to their fathers. Not one remained. And of all the Congregationalist ministers of Boston of this period, there was not so much as one who was distinguished as a pulpit orator, and who stood forth prominently as a preacher of those evangelical doctrines held by the Puritan fathers, and who could now sympathize with Lee in his mission, and extend to him the right hand of fellowship. Was it not singular indeed that these now almost forgotten doctrines should suddenly find an able and powerful advocate in this stranger from Virginia, and a follower of Wesley? .

Of the Episcopal churches, there was Christ's Church, Salem street, constituted in 1723; and their present

pulpit efficiency, he was their superior. He was stationed in Boston in 1802 and 1803; and the church under his care during these years increased from sixty to two hundred and nineteen, — a gain of almost four hundred per cent. — General Minutes, vol. i. pp. 104, 10, 18. Perhaps it could be further shown that the great revival which gave rise to the Park-street Church did not have its origin in the Baptist churches, but in the little Methodist Church in Methodist alley, under Mr. Lyell. The venerable Epaphras Kibby, now living in Chelsea, was Mr. Lyell's colleague in 1803; and the venerable Thomas Patten, of the Bromfield-street Church, joined the society during this same revival, in the spring of 1804. Mr. Lyell subsequently joined the Protestant Episcopal Church, was made a Doctor of Divinity, and died at a very advanced age a few years ago, being then rector of Christ's Church, New York, and the oldest pastor in that city at the time of his death.

house of worship, in which Charles Wesley had preached, was erected the same year: also, Old Trinity, Summer street, constituted in 1734, and its house of worship, a large wooden structure without a tower, built the following year. But of the spiritual condition of these churches at this period, we know nothing. King's Chapel, Tremont street, was constituted in 1686, and was the oldest Episcopal Church in New England. Its house of worship, yet standing, was built in 1754.* As all three of these churches were forsaken by their pastors in the exodus of the British troops in 1776, the congregation at King's Chapel took a talented and promising young man, Mr. J. Freeman, afterwards honored with a doctorate, and put him into the pulpit and reading-desk, and who continued with them during the stormy period of the Revolution. Upon his applying for ordination, after its close, to one of the newly consecrated bishops of the Protestant Episcopal Church, he having imbibed the Arianism so prevalent in Boston at that time, it was promptly refused him. Upon this, his congregation, led by their church officers, on a Sabbath afternoon in November, 1787, ordained him, under the statute of Massachusetts made and provided for such cases, left the Episcopal communion, and have never since returned. A highly opulent and respectable congregation, the representatives of former generations, yet meet there.

Thus the Episcopalians had one less church than half a century before. There was no addition to the number of Episcopal churches from 1734 to 1818, when St. Matthew's Church, South Boston, was constituted, — a period of eighty-four years! Was it superfluous that

---

* The chaste and beautiful Ionic portico which adorns its front was not added till 1789, and Washington, who was in Boston in October of that year, contributed to its erection.

the doctrines of the Thirty-nine Articles should now find in Boston an eloquent advocate in one who had been brought up in the Church of England, and who had received a portion of his earliest religious training from the apostolic Jarratt of Virginia ?*

Of the Baptist churches, the First was constituted in 1664. Its first members suffered much persecution for conscience' sake. Their house of worship, a large, plain wooden building, stood in a yard in Salem street. The Rev. Samuel Stillman, D. D., had become its pastor in 1765, as successor to the Rev. Jeremiah Condy. He was pious, talented, eloquent, and evangelical, and was eminently popular and successful. His name was long respectfully cherished by the old residents of Boston.

The Second Church, constituted in 1746, also stood in Salem street, further north. This same year that Lee entered Boston, Dr. Thomas Baldwin became the pastor of this church, and which had long been in a state of great feebleness and depression. Dr. Baldwin remained its pastor till his death, in 1825. He soon became " a tower of strength " among the Baptists, not only in Boston, but almost throughout New England. His " good name " is still " as ointment poured forth " among his brethren. These two were the only clergymen of any prominence in Boston, at this period, who fully and boldly preached the evangelical doctrines, and were able to promote revivals of religion. And yet the next addition to the number of the Baptist churches in Boston was not until 1806, when the late Dr. Sharp's, in

* The Rev. Dr. Hawkes has contributed a well-written though not complete history of the Protestant Episcopal Church in Virginia, and also a still better volume on the history of that church in Maryland. Bishop White, in his Narrative, although possessing no literary merit whatever, has also afforded us much valuable information respecting the history of that church in the United States during his own times; and I have met with some exceedingly able and well-written historical articles in the Church Review of New Haven. But it has not been my good fortune to meet with anything of importance relating to the history of Episcopacy in New England.

Charles street, was built; making a distance of time of sixty years between the second and the third.

The First Universalist Church, before mentioned, stood on the site of the present church on the corner of Hanover and Bennet streets. The Rev. John Murray was its pastor. He was an Englishman by birth; had been a member of one of Mr. Wesley's societies in Ireland, where he resided when young, and subsequently of one of Mr. Whitefield's societies in London. After adopting the doctrine of Restorationism, as taught by Relly, he came to this country the year of the death of Mr. Whitefield, in 1770, and, after various changes of fortune, became pastor of this congregation about 1785. He may be esteemed the father of American Universalism, although his followers have so transmuted the doctrine, as taught by him, that it is no longer the same thing. He was a man of popular talents, of a kind and genial spirit, and long cherished kindly feelings towards his old friends, the Methodists, and to whom, on one occasion especially, he rendered substantial aid. But his autobiography, however, for a man of his historic position, is a very unsatisfactory production.

The Sandemanian Chapel, which had been built before the Revolution, and which was the principal scene of Mr. Black's successful labors in 1785, as before narrated, stood in the rear of Hanover street. The society, always small and feeble, became extinct about the year 1823, and their house of worship was converted into a primary school.

A small Quaker meeting-house and cemetery, also, occupied a site on the west side of Congress street, now occupied by a type and stereotype foundry. The society, however, we believe, became extinct about this time.

" The first Roman Catholic congregation was assem-

bled in Boston in 1784, from the few French and Irish
then resident there, by the Abbe La Poitrie, a chaplain
in the French navy. In 1788, they obtained possession
of the old French church in School street, which had
again become vacant by the death of the Rev. Andrew
Croswell," whose congregation had occupied it for thirty-
seven years. " The first mass was performed in it Nov.
2, 1788." *

From the foregoing, it may be seen that the first half
of the last century was the period of the greatest church
extension in Boston. From 1714 to 1748, a period of
but thirty-four years, ten new churches were gathered,
and ten new houses of worship were built. For the
next half century, no new churches were formed till
towards its close, while four churches became extinct.

Such was the array of ecclesiastical force presented
by the ancient town of Boston when Lee entered it, resolved to plant a Methodist Church in its midst.

The day after his arrival was the Sabbath; and having no house in which to preach, and the season being
too far advanced for preaching on the Common, during
a part of the day he went to hear a Universalist, but
did not relish his discourse. In the evening he preached
to a company in a private house.

" The following part of the week," says he, " I met
with great and heavy trials. I took much pains to obtain a house in which to preach, but all in vain. A few
of the friendly people made a little move also, but did
not succeed. One of the greatest friends I had in town,
when I was here before, did not come to see me now,
and, when I went to see him, scarcely took any notice
of me. I met with difficulties and troubles daily; yet I
put my trust in God, and, in general, was confirmed in

* Snow's History of Boston, p. 340.

6

the opinion that God would bless my coming to Boston. I spent one evening with Mr. John Carnes, merchant, who treated me with great politeness, and said that he would assist me in anything he could. The greater part of the week was rainy, so that I went out but little. My cry was, ' Lord, help me ! ' "

Lee was a Virginian by birth; like many of the earliest Methodist preachers, had been brought up in the Church of England, and was converted in the first great revival in Virginia, under the labors of the Rev. Devereux Jarratt, and the first Methodist preachers who entered that State. He joined the itinerancy in 1783, at the close of the War of Independence; and in 1785, in connection with Bishop Asbury and the Rev. Henry Willis, assisted to introduce Methodism into Charleston, S. C. From information which he received from a young man from New England, with whom he met in this journey to the South, he long cherished a desire to visit it, and the previous year, at his own earnest request, was sent to plant Methodism on the soil of the Puritans. And it is now worthy of notice, that this man, who was esteemed the best every-day preacher in a body of men, some of whom Dr. Coke (no mean judge) pronounced the ablest preachers whom he had ever heard, either in Europe or America ; who preached the gospel from the St. Johns to the St. Marys, and with a success that has never been surpassed since the days of Whitefield ; who was once a prominent candidate for the Episcopacy, and who was able to command a tie vote for the office of Bishop, even with the apostolic Whatcoat for a competitor ; who was the first historian of American Methodism, and for several years a chaplain to Congress; who possessed an executive ability rarely surpassed, and which was especially displayed in laying in New England the foundation of that sect which even there is already the second in numerical strength, and the first in progress; who has been honored with two biographies, one of which, especially, is one of the ablest which has ever appeared from the American press;* and a man who possesses a far more distinguished place in the ecclesiastical annals of our country than any man then in the town of Boston, — received not the least notice from any minister then in it: and, with a manly independence which he ever displayed, neither does he seem to have sought it. They knew not who was among them, and neither did they care. But the results of his mighty and successful labors are now everywhere apparent.

But while thus contending with these discouragements in Boston, a few days after his arrival he received a letter from Mr. Benjamin Johnson, a respectable citizen of Lynn, inviting him to that ancient town, and to which he immediately repaired. Here an entirely different scene awaited him. He was received with the greatest cordiality: large numbers at once attended his preaching, and received the Word with all readiness of mind. And on the 20th of the following February, a class of eight persons was formed; and in a week, twenty-one more were added to their number, — the nucleus of one of the most flourishing Methodist communities on the globe; and a house of worship was built the next June. Thus success crowned the labors of the year.

But upon Mr. Lee's return to Boston, there was still no opening for him. Application had been made for a certain school-house, and also for the old court-house, but without success. But as he could not be idle, the remainder of the Conference year was devoted not only

---

* Life and Times of Rev. Jesse Lee, by the Rev. Leroy M. Lee, D.D. 8vo. pp. 519. Louisville, Ky. John Early. 1848.

to Lynn, but also to Salem, Marblehead, Danvers, Beverly, Cape Ann, Ipswich, Manchester, and Hamilton, — all in the County of Essex. In Salem, he found admission not only to the pulpit of the Rev. Joshua Spaulding, of the Tabernacle Church, before mentioned, but also to that of the Rev. Dr. Hopkins, the predecessor of the present venerable Dr. Emerson, of the South Church, in that town.

In 1791, as no place of worship was yet to be had in Boston, no special appointment was made for that place; but the Rev. John Bloodgood and Menzies Rainor were appointed for Lynn, and to which Boston was attached, as in a circuit; while Lee had the care of the whole of the infant cause in New England.

Finally, even the sterile soil of Boston bore fruit; and on the 13th of July, 1792, a class was formed at the house of Mr. Samuel Burrill, on Sheafe street, at the " North End;" and at the next Conference, — the first held in Lynn, and where so many have since met, — fifteen members are reported as in society. Who formed this class, whether Mr. Lee, or one of the circuit preachers, we are nowhere informed. The male members for the first year were Samuel Burrill, Elijah and Daniel Lewis, Abraham Ingersoll, Uriah Tufts, and Jacob Hawkins. The latter was a young Englishman, and an exhorter and local preacher of great piety and usefulness, and who was one of the first to introduce Methodism on the Cape, where it has since flourished with such eminent success, and which was in Truro. He soon died of the consumption, contracted by his severe labors on the Cape; his sun going down at noon, quenched in the darkness of death. Himself and the Rev. Joseph Snelling, yet living, and who joined in the summer of 1793, and the late Col. Amos Binney, and who joined in 1794, were band mates. One of the female members of this

original class, Mrs. Green, even at this distance of more
than sixty-seven years, yet survives, and was present
at the late celebration of the sixtieth anniversary of
the laying of the corner-stone of the first Methodist
church in Boston, held at the Hanover-street Church
Aug. 28th, 1855.

In 1792, Jeremiah Cosden was appointed to Boston.
Mr. Cosden was a gentleman of fortune, and had been
educated a lawyer; but he had left the study of Coke
and Blackstone for that of Wesley and Fletcher, and
practice in the courts, for the toils and successes of a
Methodist itinerant. One of the North End school-
houses was now obtained as a place of worship; but
morning meetings being held, in accordance with the
usages of primitive Methodism, some of the staid citizens of the neighborhood complained that their morning slumbers were disturbed by the sound of the bell
calling the humble worshippers to their devotions at
this early hour; and they were summarily ejected from
the place, — sleep being esteemed, in this case, as pref-
erable to prayer. They then obtained the use of "an
upper room" in the house of Mr. John Ruddock, on the
corner of Ship and Ann streets, opposite Clark's ship-
yard, and which, in consequence, was nicknamed "The
College." Here the apostolic Asbury once preached, on
one of his tours of Episcopal visitation to the Eastern
States, but not with satisfaction to himself; for he com-
plains of the incommodiousness of the room within, and
the disturbance of "the Jack tars and boys" without.
But yet, even in this obscure and humble temple, not
only Asbury and Lee, but also such men as Geo. Pickering, Ezekiel Cooper, John Hill, and others whose honored names are now conspicuous in the annals of American Methodism, held forth the Word of Life to the
perishing.

Finally, Aug. 28th, 1795, the corner-stone of the first Methodist church in Boston was laid, amid the rejoicings of the few and humble friends of the cause. This house, which was of wood, 36 by 46 feet in dimensions, and two stories high, with galleries, was situated in Methodist Alley, now Hanover Avenue, a most obscure place in the north part of the town. Forty members only are reported as in society at this time. The Rev. John Harper, an Irishman, who had formerly been a Wesleyan missionary in the West Indies, and who, in company with the Rev. Mr. Kingston, also a missionary, had lately arrived in New London, for the recovery of their health, which had seriously suffered in that tropical climate, was the pastor of the church at this time. They were both present at the little Conference which was held in New London the preceding month, by whose members they were most cordially and hospitably received, and from which Mr. Harper had taken this appointment. He was the father of the late Chancellor Harper, of South Carolina, in which State he subsequently located, and settled. His honored name is inseparably associated with the annals of Methodism in the Palmetto State, as well as in New England and in the West Indies.

The house went up slowly, but was finally dedicated, amid the thanksgivings and grateful tears of the infant church, by the Rev. George Pickering, on the 15th of May, 1796, by a sermon founded upon Hag. ii. 19, — "From this day I will bless you." Those who knew the man, may well suppose what the sermon was, upon this occasion. The text was eminently prophetic. But even now, the house was but partially finished, and uncomfortably furnished, and many debts embarrassed it; and it was not until 1800 that it could be said to be

completed.* The present splendid accommodations of
this church contrast strangely with its humble accommodations at this period; and why, therefore, should
men " despise the day of small things ? "

Several of the residents of the town, also, kindly assisted in this enterprise, among whom was the opulent
widow of the late Gov. Bowdoin, then residing at the
" Mansion House," in Milk street. She had a brother in
England, who was a Methodist, and a personal friend of
Mr. Wesley, in consequence of which she felt a lively
interest in the infant society, very politely received the
applicants on the occasion, Joseph Snelling and Elijah
Lewis, and wished them prosperity.

Mr. Harper, also, formed an agreeable acquaintance
with the Rev. John Murray, who, as before said, had
once resided in Ireland, where he had been a member
of a Wesleyan society; and which soon grew into a
personal attachment. Mr. Murray, therefore, generously
offered him the use of his house, in which to preach a
sermon in behalf of the new church; and in giving out
the appointment, he said to his people: " My Father's
children are coming here this evening. I wish all to
attend. And be sure that your pockets are not empty."
Mr. Murray participated in the exercises of the occasion. " We had a crowded house, and a liberal contribution," says one who was present, and who was one of
the Board of Trustees of the little church.†

Lee, also, with his characteristic zeal and devotion to
the interests of the cause, begged money for them in
New York, Philadelphia, Baltimore, on the eastern shore
of Maryland, and in the State of Delaware, — in all, to
the amount of about $520. This was, indeed, but a

---

* Stevens' Memorials of Methodism in New England.

† Rev. Joseph Snelling. See his Life, p. 21.

small sum in itself; but as great and small are relative terms, it was wealth to them, in their poverty and feebleness. It is worthy of notice, in passing, that, when the society vacated this house for their more spacious and elegant edifice in North Bennet street in 1829, and the Boston Port Society — of which the late Mr. William True, father of Dr. True of the Wesleyan University, was one of the earliest and most prominent members — purchased it for a Seamen's Bethel, and placed the Rev. E. T. Taylor in it, as chaplain, they sent him down into the same cities, to beg money to pay for it. Thus the South twice contributed to pay for that house. I remember being present at the anniversary of the Port Society, held in Dr. Channing's Church in Federal street on a cold night in January, 1832, when this fact was mentioned; and of hearing two intelligent and respectable looking gentlemen, who sat near me, express their surprise — and, as I thought, not unmixed with mortification — that Boston should be indebted to Baltimore, even, for money to assist in paying for one of its houses of worship! It was at this meeting, and which was not a large one, that that immense and enthusiastic interest in behalf of Mr. Taylor and his important enterprise was excited in the public mind, and which immediately resulted in the erection of the present commodious Bethel in North Square; and which interest, both in the man and his good work, has never flagged to this day, — a period of twenty-seven years. "May his shadow never grow less," and his work never decrease!

Of the subsequent history of Methodism in Boston, it is not my purpose to speak. Suffice it to say, that its present force consists of ten churches, with a membership of 2,500. It is also proper to say, that all the flourishing Methodist churches in the vicinity — as those of Charlestown, Chelsea, Cambridge, Roxbury, and Dorchester — arose out of the churches in the city. To God be all the glory. Amen.

As Boston is the political capital of the leading State in New England, and the commercial metropolis of the whole, so Boston Methodism is inseparably connected with the rise and progress of Methodism in all the New England States, and, for more than half a century especially, has ever exerted a powerful influence upon its character and destiny; and a notice of the whole, therefore, will not be considered out of place upon this occasion.

There are now within its bounds six entire annual Conferences, —

Having a membership of . . 81,000
Vermont and Massachusetts west of the Green Mountains, and Connecticut west of the River, belong to the Troy, New York, and New York East Conferences, which have their centres out of New England, and which portions have a membership of . . . 22,000

Making an aggregate of . . 103,000

Travelling preachers, by estimate . 885
Churches, i. e., houses of worship . 730
Parsonages 290

The value of this church property is $2,828,000*

* This gives a population of 400,000 dependent upon us for religious culture, and which is equal to the whole State of Connecticut, and which makes us the second denomination in New England in numerical strength, and the first in progress. And all this has been done in less than seventy years.

Our educational force is represented by one university, one theological school, two female colleges, and
eight first-class academies. Our religious periodical lit-
erature is represented by one able weekly, with 12,000
subscribers. The reason why we have but one is, that
we think it far better to have *one* first-class sheet, with
12,000 subscribers, than four or five little sheets with
2,000 or 3,000 only. There is also one able monthly,
devoted wholly to the subject of Christian holiness, with
a list of 12,000 more, and which has a circulation
throughout the United States, the British Provinces,
and even in England, and which is published by one of
our ministers. We have also one book-depository, the
property of the church, located in this city, under the
charge of J. P. Magee, and which is doing a prosperous
business. If it is asked, why we have but one depository
for all New England, I answer, that all the western sec-
tion of these States does business directly with the Concern in New York, while the trade of the Boston Depository is confined to the eastern portion; also the fact
that the Methodists do not confine their purchases to
their own Concern. They buy good books wherever
they can find them. Hence, you go into the library of
a Methodist preacher, and you find selections culled
from the catalogues of all the great publishers in the
land. And these facts are well known to those publishers themselves, if not to others; and hence they adver-
tise largely in Methodist periodicals. Whereas, you
rarely see a Methodist book advertised in any other
sheet; and of the 3,500,000 volumes annually issued
from our press in New York alone, — consisting of com-
mentaries, books of divinity, sermons, works on biblical
criticism, biographies, histories, and miscellaneous, and
some of which are from the first writers of the age, —

but few ever find their way into the hands of any outside of our own pale. And hence, the lamentable ignorance — at the display of which we hardly know whether, most, to weep or laugh — respecting our doctrines,
history, and especially our polity, and which is so often
displayed even by men of education and standing. We
should feel most heartily ashamed to be as ignorant of
our neighbors, as our neighbors are ignorant of us.

But this showing is far from exhibiting the whole of
New England Methodism. We have sent men and
money to build up the cause, and to promote the ad-
vance of Christianity and civilization, especially in the
great States of the Northwest, and in our rising empire
on the Pacific coast; and everywhere, from the lofty
summits of the Alleghanies to the waves of the Pacific,
New England Methodists may be found occupying posts
of usefulness and honor.

But this, even, is not all. Methodist converts are
counted by scores in the ministry of other churches,
and by thousands in their memberships; and thus the
leaven of Methodism has been diffused through the entire mass of the New England churches. Thus, while
these churches have stoutly repelled our doctrines and
our usages, by inviting our ministers and members to
their communion, they have strangely undone their own
work. It was the complaint of Bishop Asbury, fifty
years ago, that he not only had to furnish men to sup-
ply his own districts and circuits, but also the pulpits of
other denominations. Well, if they are content, so are
we. We thus do our work more thoroughly and com-
pletely.

We have also engrafted the revival system upon the
Puritan churches of New England. Those who suppose
that the revival system is a part of Puritanism, are

greatly mistaken. It has ever been quite foreign to it till recently. There were a few revivals during the first settlements of the country, and among the first generation in New England; but none again occurred until the great awakening of 1740, — a period of a hundred years; and that was mostly through the labors and influence of a Methodist, a member of the original Oxford Godly Club, and a pupil and friend of the Wesleys. And that revival in Massachusetts was put down in a very short time, not only by the influence of the press and the pulpit, but also by the exercise of church discipline; and in Connecticut it was put down by the strong arm of the law. Even the learned and saintly Edwards, under whose labors the work had commenced at Northampton, after ten long years of persecution and strife with his people, was driven from them, with a large and dependent family; and there not being a church in New England that would invite him to its pastorate, nor a college that would invite him to the vacant chair of a professorship, this ablest mind and most profound thinker whom New England ever produced, and of whom she can boast, was compelled, in his declining age, to take refuge among the frontier settlers and Stockbridge Indians, upon the western borders of civilization, where, in the midst of poverty and obscurity, he produced those works which have alike made both him and New England theology, immortal.

Revivals a part of the system of New England Congregationalism — indeed! So think the verdant ones. But if any one wishes to be informed upon this subject, which I have not time to discuss upon this occasion, let him read Hodge's "Constitutional History of the Presbyterian Church," Tracy's "Great Awakening," and, above all, the sad and mournful story of "The Life of

Jonathan Edwards," by Dr. Dwight, and I think that this man will stand corrected in this opinion. The same remarks, also, may be made respecting the great revival in Kentucky in 1799, and the years following. The Presbyterians of the West proved themselves as utterly incapable of conducting that great work to a happy and successful issue as did the Puritans of New England sixty years before, and thus ran it into the ground in like manner.

The revival system, which has so blessed the American churches for the past sixty years, and which now especially pervades the land with its blessed influence, and is assuming increasing importance every day, is the product of Methodism alone; and which, after a long and desperate struggle, it has forced upon the churches holding to evangelical doctrines, and which are alone capable of it. And for this we give glory to our common and divine Master, and in our great work "thank God and take courage."